Investi GATORS

written and illustrated by

John Patrick Green

with color by **Aaron Polk**

MACMILLAN CHILDREN'S BOOKS

For my only brother, Bill.

And my other brother, Dave.

First published 2020 by First Second

This edition published in the UK 2020 by Macmillan Children's Books
an imprint of Pan Macmillan
The Smithson, 6 Briset Street, London EC1M 5NR
EU representative: Macmillan Publishers Ireland Ltd, 1st Floor,
The Liffey Trust Centre, 117–126 Sheriff Street Upper
Dublin 1, D01 YC43
Associated companies throughout the world
www.panmacmillan.com

ISBN 978-1-5290-5437-8

5 7 9 8 6

A CIP catalogue record for this book is available from the British Library.

Cover design by John Patrick Green and Andrew Arnold
Interior book design by John Patrick Green
Interior color by Aaron Polk

Printed in Scotland

MIX
Paper from
responsible sources
FSC® C116313

Chapter 1

INVESTIGATORS

ARE ON THE CASE!

MANGO & BRASH

Mango! Get offa my case!

Oh. Sorry, Brash.

Our new **V.E.S.T.***s are in this **S.U.I.T.****case, along with our next undercover assignment!

*Very Exciting Spy Technology **Special Undercover Investigation Teams

2

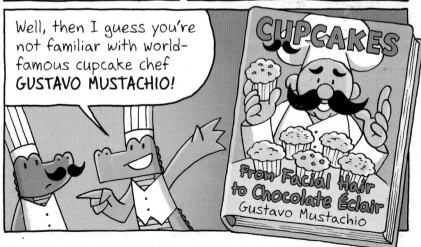

6

INVESTIGATORS! Your assignment is to go under-cover at **Batter Down**, the bakery owned by this man: world-famous cupcake chef **Gustavo Mustachio.**

AH-HA! I was right!

You might also recognize him from, like, every pizza box ever.

AH-HA! I was **ALSO** right!

QUIET, you two! Chef Gustavo has gone *MISSING!*

Mustachio hasn't been seen in **TWO WEEKS!** We suspect foul play. Batter Down was about to unveil his latest culinary masterpiece.

Someone must be after his secret recipes!

Or **maybe** some nefarious villain needs an expert baker and/or mustache model.

twirl

Hey, anything's possible.

Chapter 2

Are we supposed to pretend to be Gustavo with this mustache?

No one who really **knows** him will fall for it.

But I've learned S.U.I.T. likes its agents to be prepared for **anything**.

Maybe wearing it will trick the culprit into revealing themselves?

Do **YOU** want to wear it?

It could be your "Brash 'stache."

That's okay, Mango. I think the look has grown on you.

GROWN on me? Does this mean I have to learn how to **shave?!**

Since we don't know what S.U.I.T. wants us to do with the mustache, maybe it's best if you just take it—

Is this it? Why is the mascot a duck?

BATTER DOWN

HOT FRESH

OPEN

Right through here, to the Batter Down kitchen!

And now, if you'll get out the recipe, I can assemble the ingredients with the chef's permission.

You heard Junior Assistant Baker Marie. Hand over the recipe!

Well, it's a good **THINK** you have a backup!

I do?

In your **BRAIN**, silly! Don't you **REMEMBER** the recipe?

noogie noogie

Yes! How right you are, Junior Assistant Baker Marie. Now, leave Chef Gustavo alone so the maestro can find his muse. I'll stay here for, um...legal purposes.

What are you doing? If I'm gonna remember this recipe, I'm gonna need my assistant!

Mango, we're here to find out what happened to the **REAL** Gustavo, remember? You're **NOT** Gustavo!

Oh, right...

TAG! **YOU'RE GUSTAVO!**

slap

Hee hee! Brash 'stache.

This is serious, Mango. Now let's look for clues.

I do look pretty cool, though.

I heard that!

Sometime earlier, in a cool, dark place...

I h-h-have another b-b-batch ready...

Hmm...

...no...

ksh

ksh

...WEAK! This is no good!

CRUSH

That's just the way the cookie crumbles!

You're no baker! You're a FOOL!

23

Chapter 3

Find anything yet, Mango?

Nope. Nothing suspicious so far on this security cam footage.

Ya know, I bet Junior Assistant Baker Marie is in on it. It's **always** an inside job!

Maybe. You'd better go interrogate her.

Right! **INTERROGATOR MODE ON!**

Voop! Voop! Voop!

That's not a thing! You're just making noises!

Hey, you do things your way, I'll do things my way!

Oy, that Mango can be so frustrating!

But I guess he's an okay partner. I just don't want anyone to get hurt again.

Is he ready to hear what happened the **last** time I went undercover at a bakery?

Or, more important, am **I** ready to tell him what happened to my **LAST PARTNER...?**

SHIVER!

Meanwhile, across town, something totally unrelated is going down at the **Science Factory!**

ELECTRIC AVE.

SCIENCE FACTORY

Inside, where all the science is made, the **Head Scientist** is about to reveal their latest scientific breakthrough to the world!

Okay, okay, settle down.

Spotlight, please!

Fellow scientists! I've gathered you here to witness the unveiling of our latest scientific breakthrough, the **THINGAMABOB—**

IS IT BOB'S IDEA?

BOB'S idea? No, of course not! It's just **called** the Thingamabob. The breakthrough is—

It's broken!

BROKEN?!

WHAT?

The breakthrough is **BROKEN?**

Who broke the breakthrough?

I bet it was Bob!

RILE UP! RILE UP!

Stop it! Stop riling up! You're scientists, behave like it!

Soooo, the breakthrough is only **slightly** broken. We'll have it fixed in a jiffy!

A "jiffy" is not a precise unit of measurement!

Neither is "slightly"!

BOO!

BOO!

But we've already got a dozen reporters here for this!

Nope! It's just me. Cici Boringstories, *Action News Now.*

What? Only **one** reporter showed up for this?

And my cameraman, if he counts.

I think we all know that he does **NOT** count.

Hey! I know how to count just as high as any of you **eggheads**!

GASP!

You apologize to Dr. Doodledoo **RIGHT. NOW.**

Uh...sorry...Dr. Doodledoo... for calling you an egghead.

S'all right, bruh!

Now, then! While the breakthrough gets unbroken, what say we move the festivities outside?

It's a nice day out, and we're all a bit antsy from being **cooped up—**

GLARE!

I mean, **STUCK**—inside!

You there! Stop running around like a headless chicken! You know that's insensitive to Dr. Doodledoo!

Sorry!

Wow! This breakthrough is even more newsworthy than I thought. We should call in the chopper!

You heard it here first, viewers! A Code Sunburn has emptied the Science Factory...

...and a valuable Thingamabob sits unguarded inside, just waiting to be revealed!

NEWS

Hmm...

CTRONICS

Heh heh heh...

Chapter 4

Stay tuned for more on *Action News Now!*

BOR-ING.

I wanna ask you some questions, **Marie**. If that even is your **REAL NAME!**

It's Junior Assistant Baker Marie. And your name was Brash?

Mango—

MUSTACHE!

Oh! The **Mango Mustache!**

That's one of our top-selling fruit-filled croissants.

Don't you wish **you** could come up with such amazing recipes, Mister Brash?

nom nom

Brath ith hith firtht name. Wait—**latht** name?

Your name is "Brash Brash"?

I'm Mango.

Gulp

NO, WAIT! **HE'S** Mango. **NO!** He's GUSTAVO! Because he has the **MUSTACHE! I'M** Brash!

Now, then! When I, Brash—NO, Gustavo Brashstachio— NO, **GUSTAVO MUSTACHIO**—went missing for two weeks, did you, Marie, think to alert anyone?

Alert?

Oh, the **Red Alert!** That's our red velvet cupcake topped with a jalapeño pepper.

It's like a five-alarm fire in your mouth!

Have a bite!

No thanks, I'm full.

Aw, just one bite.

That's okay.

One. Little. Bite.

Uh...

A customer! Saved by the bell!

SPLAT!

Welcome to Batter...Down?

What does that even mean?

I have a special order for a birthday cake.

Oh, a **special** order. Chef Gustavo will handle this **personally**.

Gustavo, that's me— **I MEAN**—that's the other guy!

Wow, this cake you want is **HUGE**! You could fit a dinosaur in this thing.

CAKE
10'
HAPPY
BIRTHDAY
SCIENTIST
HUMAN for SCALE

Yes. And make it snappy.

We're alligators. **SNAPPY** is what we do best!

I MEAN—I'll get this to Chef Gustavo right away!

BRASH! Junior Assistant Baker Marie is onto us!

What? How? Did she reveal anything about Gustavo's disappearance?

Well...no. She's either a criminal mastermind or completely clueless.

But **whichever** she is, we've got to bake this special order or our cover is blown!

Hmm, that might be tough.

This cake requires a **BIG** oven, and I just discovered a **BIG** clue...

The **BIG OVEN** is missing!

Oh no!

Right? Clearly its disappearance must have something to do with **Gustavo's** disappearance.

No, I mean, how are we gonna bake this cake now?!

InvestiGators, bakin' a cake!

Is it even a thing that they know how to make?

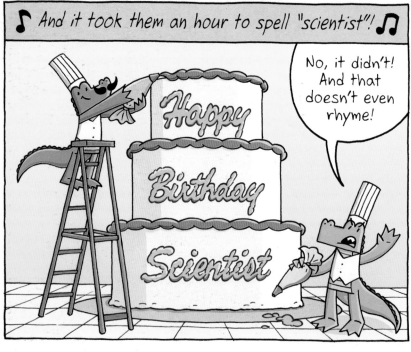

Hey, that wasn't too hard. Seems like you've done some baking before, Brash.

!

What? NO! I've never baked anything!

≥Ahem≥ Now, get back out there, **Gustavo**, and keep an eye open for anything suspicious!

I will! Good thing there's nothing suspicious about baking a giant cake for a large, mysterious figure wearing a raincoat on a sunny day!

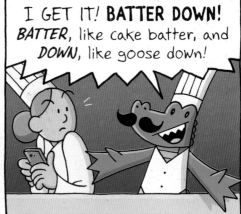

47

Cici Boringstories here, reporting outside the Science Factory. With me is **SCIENTIST BOB.** Tell us, Bob, what's this scientific breakthrough you're cooking up inside?

Ha ha! I won't tell you what **I'M** cookin', Susan, but I **will** tell you it'll blow this breakthrough—

bleep blurp

'Scuse me...

U done yet?

Need more time.

They're on 2 me :{

Sorry, Sophie. Scientist Bob's gotta motor!

Well, **that** wasn't informative **at all.** Sooooooo let's check in with the *Action News Now* helicopter in the sky!

49

Birthday cake for Bob.

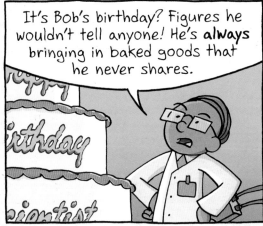

It's Bob's birthday? Figures he wouldn't tell anyone! He's **always** bringing in baked goods that he never shares.

Look at the size of that thing! I bet he's trying to steal the spotlight from today's scientific breakthrough!

So, what you want me to do with it?

Eh, leave it here. I'll deal with it later.

And...*there!* All working again!

Chapter 6

This is the *Action News Now* helicopter in the sky! An **EXPLOSION** has just **ROCKED** the Science Factory down on Electric Avenue!

AAAH!

WHAT IS IT, MARIE?!

IS IT **DANGER**?!

There's been an explosion at— Wait a minute...

...There's something different about you two...

Uh...

Ooh, an alert!

InvestiGators! Report to S.U.I.T. Headquarters *immediately!*

You know what this means...

TO THE BATHROOM!

vrrp

When ya gotta go, ya gotta go.

Mango, you **know** the quickest way to S.U.I.T. HQ is to flush ourselves into the sewer!

Oh, riiiiiiight...

NOW WHAT ARE YOU DOING??

I'M WASHING MY HANDS! **SHEESH,** how were **YOU** raised??

Are you **ready** now?

Yes.

Um...

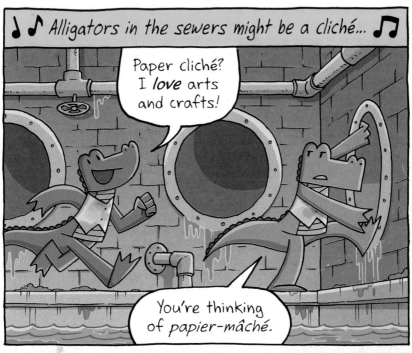

There you are!

AAH!

A floating eyeball!

Greetings, InvestiGators. I am **C-ORB**. **C**omputerized **O**cular **R**emote **B**utler.

That's new.

I may not have a nose, but I take it you arrived via your usual mode of transport?

A-yup.

stinky!

Then I will escort you to...

...**DECONTAMINATION!**

Oh, I already washed my hands—

No.

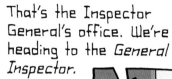

That's the Inspector General's office. We're heading to the *General Inspector.*

INSPECTOR GENERAL

Ah, I get it.

INSPECTOR VAGUE

Inspector *Vague.* Inspector *General.* Next should be Inspector *Specifi—*

INSP PAC

What? Inspector *PACIFIC?*

INSPECTOR PACIFIC

Inspector Pacific handles West Coast operations.

INSPECTOR PACIFIC

Are we there yet?

Ah, here we are—

GENERAL INFECTOR

NO! Don't go in there! Not unless you want to catch an *infectious disease!*

GENERAL INFECTOR

Oh! I see. General **INFECTOR**. That's an easy and possibly **deadly** mistake to make.

GENERAL INFECTOR

Why even **HAVE** such a room?!

Keep up, Gators!

GENERAL INFECTOR

InvestiGators! Thanks for coming so promptly. I know you're in the middle of the Gustavo Mustachio case.

Approximately **eighteen pages** ago, an explosion rocked the Science Factory down on Electric Avenue!

GOOD GOLLY, Eighteen pages! Has it really been that long?

Anyway! You're our agents nearest that location... Or, you **were**, before I ordered you to come here... But you will be **AGAIN**, once you get back there!

There's little to go on, but I have a lunch this explosion and your current investigation may be connected.

I'm sorry, **HUNCH.** I said "lunch" when I meant "hunch." I'm feeling a bit peckish.

But enough about me. Mango, Brash—it's time to SUIT up and not let S.U.I.T. down!

This way, InvestiGators. Time to get fitted for your new V.E.S.T.s!

Hey, why does Inspector *VAGUE* get two offices?

That's Inspector **VOGUE**. They handle striking poses and all manner of dance.

Okay, *VAGUE*, *VOGUE*—that's a bit of a stretch.

Indeed! It takes a **lot** of stretching to be limber enough for all those fancy dance moves.

Keep up, Gators!

FOOD COURT

PIZZA BURGERS SAMMIES

CURRY RAMEN

Ooooh...

Here we are. The A.R.M.S. division.

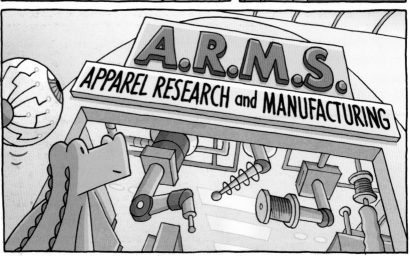

A.R.M.S.

APPAREL RESEARCH and MANUFACTURING

What's the S for?

The S is for SIX.

Hello! I'm Agent Six.

NO! No, no. *NOT* six. The S is for **SVEN!** I am Sven Septapus, lead designer of A.R.M.S.

I also have the **MOST** arms. Look at them. Look at all these arms!

Agent Six. Agent Sven.

OH! I have a *JOKE!*

Oh no.

WHY WAS SIX AFRAID OF SVEN?

Because—

...nanoscopically integrated into the thousand-thread-count weave...

...all accessible at the touch of a button!

Beep!

ZIP

FLIP

VMM

ZRRP

Ooooh...

This is great!

You liked the demonstration?

Oh, sure, but I meant this PB & PB sandwich I got at the food court.

Chapter 7

Just then, about twenty-six pages ago...

An **EXPLOSION** has just **ROCKED** the Science Factory down on Electric Avenue!

Did an experiment go wrong? It's hard to see what's happening through all the smoke...

≥Cough! Cough!≤ Is everyone all right?

Dr. Doodledoo! **NOOOOOOO!!**

I'm fine. How are you?

Ooh, you found my lunch!

Your lunch is an entire roast chicken?

Hey, doing science makes me hungry!

Uh... So, this is awkward.

Hopefully the injuries are minimal, since most of the scientists were outside.

I can see ambulance lights through the smoke now...

Woo Woo Woo

HALT! There's been a **science** accident!

We're InvestiGators.

Badges?

We're not badgers, we're alligators!

zip zip

Okay, checks out.

Did you notice anything unusual before the explosion?

There's **always** something unusual going on at this place, but let me think...

We were in the middle of a **Code Sunburn**, so everyone was outside. A guy delivered a giant birthday cake for Bob, which I wheeled inside. Then I ran into one angry scientist, who was on his phone—it said something about a *jamboree* on the screen. Don't think I've seen him since, but it can be hard to tell these scientists apart. Well, except for the chicken.

Oh, and the only **serious** injury seemed to be to the Head Scientist, who was just taken away in an ambulance.

Thanks, security dude. Keep up the good work.

"Jamboree" sounds like a code word. Maybe the **go** signal to set off the explosion?

Possibly...

...and there's something familiar about a giant birthday cake...

Mm-hmm.

Mango, you see what clues you can dig up inside. I'll talk to everyone out here.

Got it!

SCIENTISTS! My name is Brash. I'm an InvestiGator from S.U.I.T. Is everyone all right? Anyone unaccounted for?

We're all fine, just a few scrapes and bruises.

But the Head Scientist was inside during the blast!

Oh, and **Bob** is missing. But nobody likes **him**.

Bob is a scientist?

Feh! Not a *GOOD* one!

He's only been here, like, a week, and already no one can tolerate him.

Mm-hmm. Does anyone know what caused the explosion?

No. We have experiments blow up here all the time, but nothing like this! It was all, *KABLOOEY!!*

Okay, okay! It's called... THE THINGAMABOB.

As in *Scientist Bob?*

No, wait! We changed it. It's now called...THE THINGAMA**STEVE**.

It's a laser beam that digitizes actual money. It erases the *physical* cash from existence, but puts its *value* inside a computer!

DEPOSIT $200

It even works through walls! Metal, brick, wood, straw—*whatever!* Just point it wherever there's money and it's **yours!**

It basically transfers money from the real world into any bank account you want— preferably a high-interest savings account.

Why is it called the THINGAMASTEVE? Why not something like...the REVERSE ATM? Or...the DEPOSITRON? Or CASH GRAB?

Hey, we're **scientists**, not **writers**.

Well, I can see why you'd want to keep such a powerful tool safe. Pretty odd that you were going to **ANNOUNCE IT TO THE WORLD ON THE NEWS!**

AAAANYWAY... You said you haven't seen Bob since the explosion. Could **he** have taken the device? Did anyone have any of his birthday cake?

What? No one told *ME* there was cake!

Hi, there! Cici Boringstories, *Action News Now*. I interviewed Scientist Bob, but that tape got ruined in the explosion.

However, our news chopper in the sky should have caught something on camera—

Huh? Where'd it fly off to?

Uh... Thanks, Cici. I'll get to the chopper.

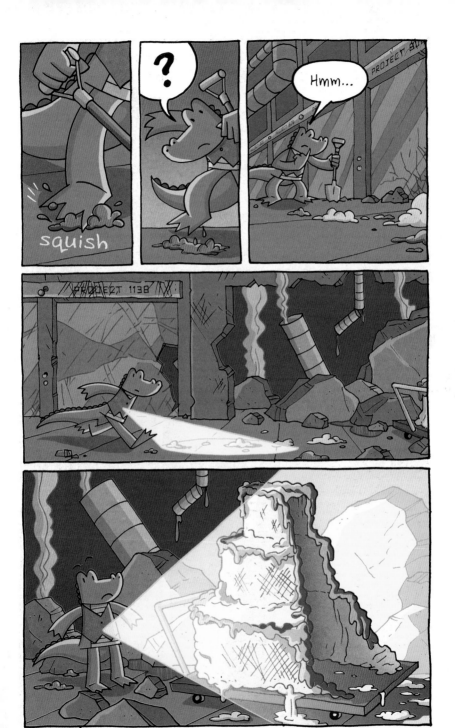

Splorp

≥GASP AGAIN!≤

Back outside...

How about the word "jamboree"? That mean anything to anyone?

It means "party," right?

Yo, somebody say "party"?

BRASH! BRASH!

WHEW! ≷huff huff huff≶

Pant Pant

Let me...catch my... breath...

chug chug chug

AAAAAH, refreshing!

WELL?!

Bob's birthday cake was right by the explosion! And it was the same cake that **WE** made! Something—or **someone**— was hidden inside it!

I **KNEW** there was something weird about those cake instructions!

And not only that—I found the **medium** oven that's missing from the bakery! It was part of something called PROJECT 808.

PROJECT 808

BAKEMEISTER 2000

Whose project is 808? Is it **yours**, you big chicken?

Nah, bruh. I try to stay away from ovens I could fit in.

Not my project, either.

Then do any of you recognize THIS MAN? It looks like his disappearance may have some connection to what's happened here.

I've seen him, bruh!

Mango, I'm going to talk to the Head Scientist at the hospital. You follow the trail of cake crumbs.

Beep

VPP VPP

It's a good thing we baked chocolate microchips into the cake. I can track them with my V.E.S.T.!

bip bip

SCIENCE FACTORY

bip bip bip bip bip

Down below...

You have everything you need to rebake me, Gustavo. This next batch better be *perfect.*

I long to be **WHOLE** again.

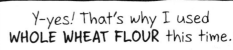

Y-yes! That's why I used **WHOLE WHEAT FLOUR** this time.

Hmm... spongy... durable...

...the crack is nice and moist...

Yes... That's a *lovely bake.*

107

Your **SUPER DOUGH** is ready, Chef Mustachio.

PREPARE THE MOLD!

This super dough will make me **harder...** *better...faster...**STRONGER!!***

At last I will reveal myself to the Gators.

At last I will have **REVENGE!**

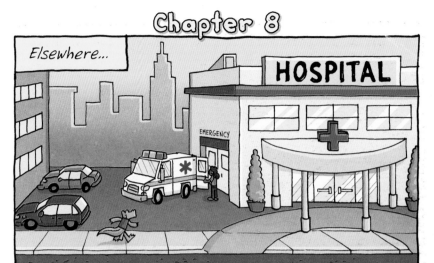

Chapter 8

Elsewhere...

HOSPITAL

EMERGENCY

All I'm saying is, I knew the way to the hospital—

Did a head scientist with a head injury come through here?

Thanks!

Hey, how could I know the GPS was gonna take us all over town?

Whoever's behind all this means *business!* I hope Mango's faring better than I am. I don't want him to get hurt...or **worse.**

We haven't been partners for long... but I just can't go through that again!

Nurse! Scalpel!

Shall I draw a dotted line to indicate where to make the incision?

No need! I'm going to **eyeball** it.

WOW! You really know how to chop a guy open! They should call you...

...the **CHOPPER!**

the **CHOPPER**

CHOPPER

CHOPPER
CHOPPER

CHOPPER

Many moons ago...

Here I am, **Jake Hardbones**, backpacking over the Scottish Highlands...

Or should I say, **DOCTOR** **Jake Hardbones**, as I'm on vacation in celebration of my graduation from **Brain Surgery School!**

AH! A village! Perhaps the townsfolk will let me pick their brains about any local legends!

Pick their brains! **HA HA!** Now that I'm a brain surgeon, I finally know what that means!

Hello! I'm not from around these parts. This seems like a place with **tales** to **tell**.

≥SIGH≤ Well—

OY!

poke!

Ya wanna hear a **STORY**, do ya?

Indeed I do!

Even *more* moons ago... travelers came to this quaint village on a **MACHINE** from the **SKY!**

It was a helicopter.

These beings **PROBED** our minds with their technology!

It was a news crew filming a piece on bed-and-breakfasts.

chop chop chop

Hoping to chase them out of town, the local mystic **CURSED** their flying contraption with **RABIES!**

That part's true.

In the dark of the lunar eclipse they got in their machine and **FLEW OFF**, never to be seen again!

They were here maybe twenty minutes.

But on nights like this, their **FLYING DEVIL** can still be heard...

And **SOME** say it haunts the hillside waiting for victims to pass its curse on to.

Who says that?

I do. I say it. I said it just now. Weren't you listening?

You were bitten pretty bad, son. You need a doctor.

I...I **AM** a doctor...

Not just a doctor anymore. You're a WERE-COPTER now.

That machine's curse is coursing through your veins. And that's **bad news.** Now, whenever there **IS** news, you will be forced to transform into a news copter to report on it.
You have become...

...DOCTOR COPTER!

NOOOOOOOOOOOOOOO

DOCTOR! The patient is flatlining!

Ope!

boop...boop...boop...

My fault...

...I knocked out the cord.

Chapter 10

Meanwhile, all over town...

...Mango is tracking the chocolate microchips.

Man, wherever this culprit went, they sure took the **long way** to get there!

You're supposed to be following the cake crumbs!

I did! The signal led me right here!

Well, not *right* here. It led me all over town—

Hold up!

If the **tracker** led you here, and the **Head Scientist** is here...

...then this **WAS** an inside job! The Head Scientist was inside the factory with the cake **AND** the invention. The cake must have been meant to sneak the invention **OUT!**

What about Bob?

Bob was **clearly** his partner, who double-crossed him, set off the explosion as a distraction, and made off with the invention for *himself!*

Hmm, I dunno...

DROP THAT BRAIN!

Um, I really shouldn't.

THIS MAN IS THE CRIMINAL! *WAKE UP!*

Guhhh

YOU were gonna steal the money-ray thing! The cake was YOUR idea! **CONFESS!**

I confess... I know it was wrong...

Ah-HA!

I ate some of the cake...even though it's not my birthday...

It's true! According to his ID, today's *not* his birthday!

And look! I sliced him open, and found a slice of cake!

If he was going to sneak the device out *in* the cake...why would he *eat* the cake?

Gimme one second...

rrr

RRRRR

POP!

Here you go!

Uh... thanks?

Now, if you'll excuse me, I have to get back to SAVING THAT MAN'S LIFE!

NURSE! Where were we?

Well, I was eating this cake...

...uh...but maybe...

...we should put back this brain?

Correct!

And who knows? If I put this brain in *juuuuust right*, maybe this scientist will be even smarter than he was before! *Ha ha ha!*

WOW! That *would* be **NEWS!**

twitch

Let's get back to the **bakery** and watch this news footage!

SURGERY >>>

Brash...? What's wrong?

Mango... This investigation has me worried that something **bad** is going to happen.

At the bakery?

Brash, we're partners. I trust you with my life. So whatever you think will happ—

Mango.

The **last** time I went undercover at a bakery... my partner...

Speaking of the sewer...

Um... If you don't mind me asking, how'd you get like this?

I DO MIND!

But now that you mention it, maybe my origin story will help you with your task.

I wasn't always a tasty treat. But I always had a taste... for **JUSTICE.**

I was once a *good guy*, Gustavo. A crocodile named Daryl. But then...a **catastrophe** changed all that!

What happened?

I fell into into a vat of **radioactive cracker dough.**

I thought I was going to die.

Instead, I became **one** with the dough.

Machines rolled me out...

...and baked me into individual saltines.

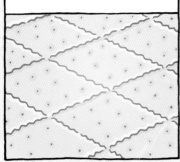

Then I was packaged, put on a truck, and shipped off to who knows where.

Inside the box I felt myself growing, thanks to the radiation.

Or maybe it was the rapid-rise yeast.

I combined with all the other *me* crackers and *BURST* through that vacuum seal, forevermore to be known as—

Crackerdaryl?

What? No. Cracker**DILE**. Because I'm a **crocodile**.

Though... Crackerdaryl *does* kinda work...

But no! If I went by Cracker**DARYL**, someone might recognize me by the name.

As Cracker**DILE**, I could be **ANY** crocodile who fell into a vat of radioactive cracker dough and came back to life!

Are...there a lotta those runnin' around?

No. I'm all alone, Gustavo.

Life since my evolution hasn't been kind.

The transformation may have granted me the **strength** of a giant saltine...

...but it also made me **weak** to moisture and hungry vermin.

Then why do you live in the sewer? It's full of both moisture *AND* vermin!

I might be the crumbling remains of a **cracker** on the outside...

...but I'm still a **crocodile** on the inside!

Well, you will crumble no more after you get inside...

...and then come *OUT* of... this baking mold!

With your **SUPER DOUGH**, I'll be invincible! Soon the world will bask in the fresh-from-the-oven heat of Crackerdile—*REBAKED!*

This will make you more of a cookie, really. Or maybe a biscuit.

Just get on with it, Mustachio!

140

Chapter 11

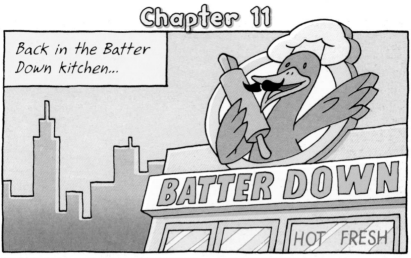

Back in the Batter Down kitchen...

Okay, here we go...

Ooh, down there!

PLAY ▶

That's the reporter interviewing one of the scientists. I didn't see him at the factory.

THAT must be Scientist Bob!

Then the cake and the guy who ordered it show up.

Now that I think about it, why **was** he in a raincoat when the sun was out?

Beats me.

And then the guard wheels the cake inside.

WAIT! Go back. *ENHANCE!*

ZOOM x3

PLAY▶

ZOOM x3

PLAY▶

ZOOM x3

PLAY▶

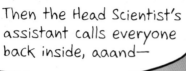

Then the Head Scientist's assistant calls everyone back inside, aaand—

—BOOM!

PLAY ▶

There's a lot of smoke. Can't make much out.

STOP! Freeze right there!

Are those...horns?

Double enhance!

TRIPLE enhance!

GIVE IT ALL THE ENHANCE!

144

That's a triceratops!

Not just *ANY* triceratops— That's **HOUDINO**, the dinosaur escape artist!

That means the guy in the raincoat...was a **hooded Houdino!** An escape artist *and* master of disguise, apparently!

Junior Assistant Baker Marie! Where's the store copy of the receipt for that giant birthday cake?

Here.

If he paid with a credit card, we can track where else he's been!

Drat! He paid cash! How are we going to find him?

BREAKING NEWS!
All over the city, money is disappearing into *thin air!*

This is Cici Boringstories in the *Action News Now* studio!

The city's banks are **EMPTY!**

MONEY GO BYE-BYE

ING REPORT — ACTION NEWS NOW — BREAKING REPORT — AC

One minute the money was there, the next it was gone. *Poof!* It's like someone has a **laser beam** that can suck up money through walls!

One thing's for sure: If your money's in a safe, your money *ISN'T SAFE!*

Great! Now there's a **CRIME WAVE!**

With that scientific breakthrough, Houdino doesn't even need to break **in** to make a break**out**!

So if Scientist Bob hired Houdino to steal that invention...how does that connect to Gustavo's disappearance?

?

OH! Uh... Which one of you is pretending to be Gustavo this time?

I MEAN—Chef Mustachio is missing again???

whaaaaat...

That's, like, so cray...

WHO DO YOU KEEP TEXTING?!

snatch!

SABBob

On way

Heat 2 hot

Stay out kitchn

SAB...Bob?

Could that be... *Scientist* Bob?

Yes! And when the guard told us Bob's phone said *jamboree*...

149

...what he *actually* saw was the name *JABMarie!* Bob was talking to **Junior Assistant Baker Marie!**

You're in cahoots with Scientist Bob!

What's he need the oven for?

Oven? What are you talking about?

The BIG oven is missing!

Medium oven.

We have, like, **SO** many ovens. You can't expect me to notice if one is missing.

You only had **THREE!**

And for some people, they're very easy to tell apart!

FORGET THAT! WHERE'S HOUDINO? WHAT HAVE YOU DONE WITH GUSTAVO?

I know nuttin' about no Houdino! And Gustavo... It was just an accident! *Honest!*

We... We saw him fall down a manhole. And instead of calling for help...we did nothing.

What do you mean, "**WE**"?

ding ding

GUSTAVO!

It's-a me!

Chef Mustachio!

I'm... I'm all right...

Well, this mystery certainly solved itself.

I guess our work here is done. **CASE CLOSED!**

*What? **No**, Mango! **NOT** case closed. There are still many threads to resolve!*

Ah! Junior Assistant Baker Marie! I'm so glad you're okay.

Um, *thanks?*

When I found myself in chains I feared the worst!

I had to bake, and bake, and bake, and bake... And I was afraid once I could bake no more, **YOU'D** be forced to suffer the same fate!

It's good to be back, and to see you're safe.

So Marie **wasn't** involved in your disappearance?

No, Marie and Bob had nothing to do with it.

Say, where is Bob?

Bob was tired of living in Chef Mustachio's mushadow. We wanted to start our own bakery together!

But **GUSTAVO** keeps all his **BEST** recipes in his **HEAD**!

What about the ones in his book?

CUPCAKES

From Facial Hair to Chocolate Éclair
Gustavo Mustachio

That book only goes up to *ÉCLAIR!* There are **twenty-one** more letters' worth of recipes after that! The only way to figure out Gustavo's secret recipes is to reverse engineer them!

But that takes more *science* than we had available to us here.

And at the Science Factory, they've got *all* the science!

THAT'S RIGHT! When Bob and I saw Gustavo fall down that manhole, it was the perfect opportunity to put our plan into action. We didn't think he was *missing*. We just thought he was stuck in that hole.

So Bob disguised himself as a scientist to blend in at the Science Factory...

...and deconstructed Gustavo's baked goods with **science** to steal his secret recipes!

THAT'S why he took the big oven!

Medium oven.

You mean *THAT* oven? No, no, that oven was with me.

But I saw it at the Science Factory!

The *Bakemeister 2000*? It's one of the three best ovens on the market! You can cook up almost **ANYTHING** in there.

I'd be surprised if the Science Factory didn't have at least one of their own.

So...was Bob working with **Houdino** or what?

Who?

Dino.

Who?

Dino.

Who?

Dino.

Who—

ENOUGH!

HE DOESN'T KNOW HOUDINO!

WHICH MEANS...the connections between Gustavo's disappearance, Bob and Marie's recipe thieving, and Houdino's cake shenanigans...

...are just coincidence?

I guess the General Inspector's lunch was wrong.

Marie, why would you steal my recipes? I thought you *liked* working at Batter Down.

I was just in it for the dough!

And by "dough," I mean *MONEY!*

And you **bumbling gators** will *never* catch Senior Assistant Baker Bob! He's too **smart** for you!

Oh, *really?*

tap tap tap

SABBob

U still their?

Coast is clear. Come back 2 bakery

Good thing I just happened to run out of the factory with these stolen recipes right before the explosion!

And with Gustavo stuck in that manhole, **BAKER BOB'S** is gonna have the **best baked goods** in the *world!!*

Marie...?

CLAMP!

Oh, dang!

Hi, Bob.

Chapter 12

That's two criminals down.

Good job, partner.

Now we've got to figure out how to catch Houdino before he robs the entire city!

That triceratops will be hard to find.

But what he couldn't escape were **low ticket sales**. So he turned to a life of crime—mostly bank robbing. He won't pass up a **steal**, and can't pass up a **deal**.

There is no vault that can stop him, and no cell that can hold him. Houdino likes to **break in**, **break out**, and **BREAKDANCE**.

Well, Mango, looks like to bust Houdino...

...we'll have to *BUST A MOVE*.

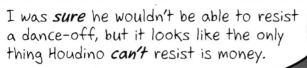

I was **sure** he wouldn't be able to resist a dance-off, but it looks like the only thing Houdino **can't** resist is money.

Even if it's small change!

The only things left in here are lint and mismatched buttons.

With that invention, robbing *anyone* is a piece of cake!

Hold up...

The Thingamasteve *ONLY* works on money. Which means Houdino can't use it to steal anything else.

Right...

So what's the money **FOR?** He hasn't been caught spending it on anything.

Maybe he's saving it for a rainy day? He's got that raincoat, after all.

Yeah, but with all that money he could **BUY** anything he wants and then use the device to **STEAL** the money back again!

That's a good point. Houdino's not just *shifty*, he's also *thrifty*!

We have to lure him out with something money *can't* buy!

...Love?

No, something that can't be sucked through walls!

OH, I see where you're going with this...

To catch this triceratops, we'll have to set a tricera-*trap!*

170

Chapter 13

And so...

I may have more money now than I could ever spend...

...but I'm not gonna pass up something that's **FREE**!

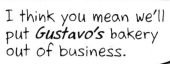

I think you mean we'll put *Gustavo's* bakery out of business.

Oh, right.

ding ding

SHUSH! This might be Houdino!

HOT

Is that him?

I can't tell with his hood up.

I'd like my free PB & PB & PB, please.

Tricera-**TRAPPED!**

You won't be stealing money with *this* anymore!

How'd you even know about this thing, Houdino?

I didn't. But when I saw on the news that all the scientists at the Science Factory were outside, I knew that place would be easy pickin's. There's **ALWAYS** some contraption that can be used for evil at the Science Factory!

Gustavo!

Gators, *please* tell me I can stop baking your crazy pastries.

I did enough of that in the sewer!

What happened to you? Start from the beginning.

Well, I was born a poor farm boy—

START from your abduction.

I was waxing my mustache while walking to work, when someone grabbed my leg and pulled me down!

?!

BATTER D

He was the most **UNSAVORY** character...though maybe he'd be all right with a sharp cheese and some prosciutto...

He was...crumbling... half-eaten...

YOU'RE NOT MAKING ANY SENSE, MAN!

He forced me to develop a new type of dough. A *super dough*. A **hybrid** of cracker, cake, cookie, and bread.

A **HYBREAD.**

Gustavo, what happened next? How did you escape?

While he was baking, I broke free of my shackles with a spoon.

And then I had to do the most horrible thing...

Crawl out of the sewer?

No. I broke the first rule of baking...

...I left while the oven was on!

You had to do what you had to do, Gustavo...

≥sob≤

It was a **LOAF**-or-death situation.

hee hee hee

≳Ahem≲ 'Scuse me.

≳SOb≲

Brash...?

You okay?

I think I know who this Crackerdile is...

Mango... It's time I told you what happened to my old partner at that bakery...

His name was Daryl. He was S.U.I.T.'s top agent! I learned so much from him in our time together.

Our assignment was supposed to be easy as pie.

Daryl was going to retire. It was his last mission.

But no one expected it to be his *last* last mission.

We were cracking down on a cracker company that was disposing of **nuclear waste** by baking it into their **saltines!**

We cracked the case...

...but there was an incident with a cat.

Daryl fell into the radioactive dough...

WHIRRRRR

glub blub

...and was never seen again.

Epilogue

Not far below...

TIMER

DING!

HA-*HAAA!*

Even if Gustavo didn't use the super dough, as a former agent of S.U.I.T., Crackerdile is still a force to be reckoned with.

Listen—we're **MANGO** and **BRASH**. We're **INVESTIGATORS!**

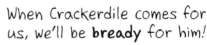

When Crackerdile comes for us, we'll be **bready** for him!

We'll get that cracker in a **jam!**

He'll be **toast!**

We'll... We'll...

We'll bring that crust to justice?

HA! Good one!

THE END...for now!

INVESTIGATORS

How to draw **MANGO** & **BRASH**

1. Draw two arches that sort of look like a bird with long, droopy wings.

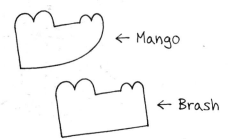

2. Add a short line for the top of the snout.

3. Draw two smaller arches for the nose.

4. Make a line at the back of the head, and for **Mango** draw a curved snout connecting his neck to his nose.

If you're drawing **Brash**, give him a rectangular snout.

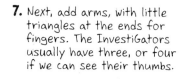

← Mango

← Brash

5. Add details like eyes, nostrils, and neck ridges. Give them expressions with their mouths and eyebrows!

6. Mango and Brash have identical bodies. Let's draw Mango's, because Brash looks grumpy!

Draw a slightly crooked box shape for the torso.

7. Next, add arms, with little triangles at the ends for fingers. The InvestiGators usually have three, or four if we can see their thumbs.

8. Draw legs and feet, similar to the arms, with three triangles for toes.

9. Add a tail.

10. Almost done! Your Gator will need belly stripes and tail ridges.

11. Remember to put them in a V.E.S.T. when they're on the job!

12. Last, give them some gadgets and color them in. Mango is dark green and Brash is light green. What kind of spy gear do **YOU** think they should have?

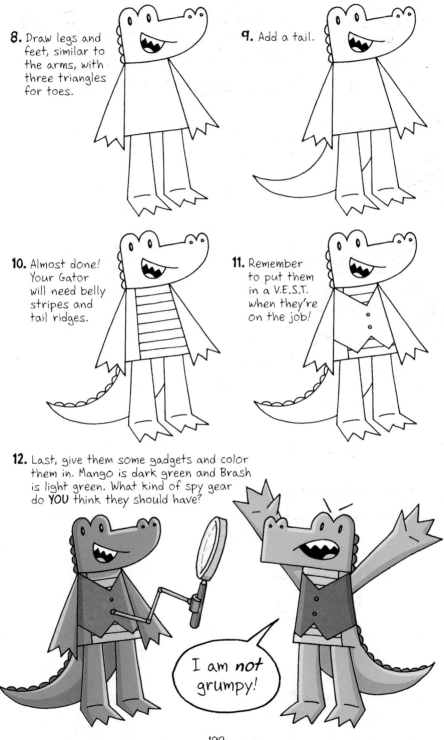

I am *not* grumpy!

AGENT SIX has a PB & PB & PB, but he can't eat it without a *mouth*! Make a photocopy of this page and draw a new face for him that shows if he thinks it will taste *delicious* or *disgusting*!

How to draw C-ORB*
*Computerized Ocular Remote Butler

1. Draw a circle.

2. Draw another circle.

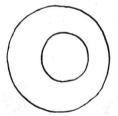

3. Draw two more circles!

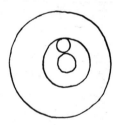

4. Draw details like circuitry and iris lines. Add little swooshes to indicate C-ORB is floating.

5. Give C-ORB arms and color if you like. Use different colors to change C-ORB's mood!

Special thanks to...

Aaron Polk and his flatters, Christine Brunson and Bobby Fasel, for their awesome colors.
Conner Tribble, for his lyrical influence.
My editors, Calista Brill and Rachel Stark, and the rest of the wonderful team at First Second Books.
My agent, Jen Linnan, for getting my jokes.
Gina Gagliano, for putting up with my jokes.
My brother, Bill, for inspiring many of my jokes.
Dave Roman, for being my brother-in-comics.
And my family, for leaving me alone in my room while I drew comics.

John Patrick Green is a human with the human job of making books about animals with human jobs, such as *Hippopotamister*, the Kitten Construction Company series, and now *InvestiGators*. John is definitely not just a bunch of animals wearing a human suit pretending to have a human job. He is also the artist and cocreator of the graphic novel series Teen Boat!, with writer Dave Roman. John lives in Brooklyn in an apartment that doesn't allow animals other than the ones living in his head.